When I Feel Sad

WRITTEN BY

Cornelia Maude Spelman

ILLUSTRATED BY

Kathy Parkinson

Albert Whitman & Company
Morton Grove, Illinois

For Tidie, who didn't know she could share it. — C. M. S.

To Katie, with love. — K. P.

Books by Cornelia Maude Spelman

After Charlotte's Mom Died ~ *Mama and Daddy Bear's Divorce*
Your Body Belongs to You

The Way I Feel Books:

When I Care about Others ~ *When I Feel Angry*
When I Feel Good about Myself ~ *When I Feel Jealous*
When I Feel Sad ~ *When I Feel Scared* ~ *When I Miss You*

Library of Congress Cataloging-in-Publication Data

Spelman, Cornelia.
When I feel sad / by Cornelia Maude Spelman ; illustrated by Kathy Parkinson.
p. cm. (The way I feel)
Summary: A young guinea pig describes situations that make her sad,
how it feels to be sad, and how she can feel better.
ISBN 0-8075-8891-1 (hardcover) ISBN 0-8075-8899-7 (paperback)
[1. Sadness — Fiction. 2. Guinea pigs — Fiction.] I. Parkinson, Kathy, ill. II. Title. III. Series.
PZ7.S74727 Wi 2002 [E] — dc21 2002001956

Published in 2002 by Albert Whitman & Company, 6340 Oakton Street, Morton Grove, Illinois 60053-2723.
Published simultaneously in Canada by Fitzhenry & Whiteside, Markham, Ontario.

Printed in China through Colorcraft Ltd. Hong Kong.
10 9 8 7 6 5 4 3 2

The design is by Scott Piehl.

For more information about Albert Whitman & Company,
please visit our web site at www.albertwhitman.com.
Please visit Cornelia at her web site: www.corneliaspelman.com.

Note to Parents and Teachers

It is painful for us when children are sad. Their sorrow makes us anxious to help them so that they can feel happy again. It also arouses our own feelings of sadness. Yet, if we didn't learn that it was okay to acknowledge and share our own unhappy feelings, we may deny or minimize our children's, or try to distract them from these feelings.

This reaction, while understandable, is not helpful. It teaches children not to pay attention to their feelings or share them with others. Children need to learn that sharing feelings with other human beings brings comfort. Some adults who did not learn this, who did not experience being understood and listened to, have problems in relationships. Others may turn for comfort to substances instead of to people.

But there is a difference between acknowledging a child's feeling, offering comfort, and overindulging. The child who is sad can be offered physical closeness, listening, and time to share his sadness, yet still be expected to pick up his toys, to carry on. It's a question of timing, of giving emotions their due before we offer activities which will help move the child past the sadness.

This book addresses ordinary sadness. We can help a child who grieves following a death or other major loss in these same ways, but we need to be attentive over a longer period of time. And when for too long a child stays sad, cries frequently, is listless, has problems eating and sleeping—seek professional help. Even very young children can suffer from clinical depression, which requires intervention.

We want our children to know that we value all of their feelings—positive or negative—that all of us, children and adults, experience such feelings, and that we know how to deal with them. We want to build our children's confidence in their coping ability, so that they will be able to say, "When I feel sad, I know I won't stay sad."

Cornelia Maude Spelman, M.S.W.

Sometimes I feel sad.

I feel sad when someone won't let me play,

or when I really want to tell about
something and nobody listens.

When someone else is sad,
I feel sad, too.

I feel sad when I want to be with somebody,

but he's not there.

If something bad happens, I feel sad.

When I can't have something I really,
really want, or when I lose something special,
I feel sad.

When someone is cross with me, I feel sad,

and I feel sad when I get hurt.

Sad is a cloudy, tired feeling.
Nothing seems fun when I feel sad.

I don't like feeling sad!
I want sadness to go away.

But everyone feels sad sometimes.

When I feel sad, there are ways to feel better.
I can tell someone I'm sad.

"That's OK," they say, and sit close to me.
It feels good to be close to someone
when I'm sad.

It's all right to show I'm sad.
It's all right to cry.

After a while, I'm done crying. But I might still want to talk about what made me sad.

Pretty soon I start to feel better. I want to go
to the park and swing on the swings.

I want to make something

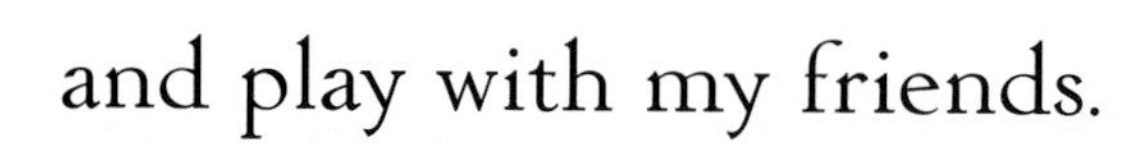

and play with my friends.

The sad feeling goes away,
and I feel good again.

When I feel sad, I know I won't stay sad!